# Lost
# in the
# Wilderness

Martin P. Van Ieperen

This title is also available as an eBook on Amazon.

Martin-van-ieperen@shaw.ca

Dedicated to my grandson, Levi Martin Mushovic.

Thanks to my wife, Gerrie, for her excellent advice and proofreading. And to my son, Taco, for his assistance in the publication.

*Luck lies in odd numbers.  - Shakespeare*

November, 2017

# Chapter 1

Exhausted she sat down on the mossy branch of a fallen evergreen tree and scanned the wilderness around her. Suddenly its vastness and silence overwhelmed her. She knew she had wandered too far from the hiking trail. Much too far! But it wasn't her fault.

Accusingly she looked at Tala, her puppy.

It was *her* doing!

Well, not quite.

Tracy's parents had given her the dog for her birthday, her fourteenth. With her white head, grey rump, and black tail ending in an impressive white plume, Tala looked like a cross between a Border Collie and a Poodle.

But was she?

Nobody really knew. But that didn't matter. Nobody cared. Tracy didn't care either. Everyone loved her just as she was. Tracy had called her Tala. It went well with her own name, she thought.

Tracy and her friend Bonny, together with their parents, were camping for a few days with a motor home on a remote site in the large *Salmon Lake Wilderness*. Early that morning the two enterprising girls had decided to walk to the lake, a 12 km easy hike. The lake was an attractive one, offering boating and several other recreational activities. Though the trail was rather primitive, not often used by hikers, the girls didn't care. They saw it as a real challenge. The weatherman was co-operated: he had promised calm winds and uninterrupted sunshine. The new puppy had to come along, of course. Not for anything in the world would the girls have left her behind!

"But keep Tala on a leash girls," their parents had told them, "you can't trust a puppy if she is unleashed. She'll run away on you!"

The parents had, of course, been rather reluctant to let them go to the lake all by themselves. But after they had extracted a promise from the two girls to be careful and not to do foolish things, they had consented. After all, Bonny was already 16 years old and a very responsible girl. And Tracy, 14 now, wasn't a small child anymore either. Very sensible like Bonny, she had never done any irresponsible thing in her whole life either.

So the two girls, after stuffing their backpacks with food, water, and other essential hiking things, and having promised (amidst loud laughter from everyone) not to get lost, had left for Salmon Lake. Tracy's dad had promised to pick them up with his truck in the evening.

After having made some very good progress during the first three hours, the girls had become a little tired, and decided to have a snack and a short rest. So they had sat down on a patch of grass, and remembering their promise, had tied Tala to a tree.

But the puppy, hadn't been happy at all with being tied to a tree! She started yapping. She wanted to be free to roam around. No wonder that the girls had felt sorry for her. So they did what they had promised their parents not to do: they had unleashed her.

Tala, of course, had loved it! Running from tree to tree, sniffing at all those things she had never seen yet nor sniffed at, she had suddenly decided that to explore the world was even more exciting than staying on the trail. After all, she had seen so little of it yet. Quietly taking off when the girls weren't looking, she had disappeared behind a dense grove of evergreens nearby.

At first Tracy hadn't thought her disappearance was a big deal.

"Puppies are inquisitive animals," she had told Bonny, "and when tired, they always come back to their owners."

But that hadn't happened.

Tala hadn't come back.

Then Tracy, getting a little worried, had tried to coach her back by loudly calling her name, even with several tonal variations, and then when *that* didn't work, had warned her loudly in no uncertain terms that she *had* to come back, or face dire consequences.

Though Tala had lukewarmly listened to her by showing her face a few times from behind a distant shrub or tree, and condescended to bark once or twice to let Tracy know where she was, Tala had refused to come back. To the consternation of the girls she then suddenly had disappeared behind some distant bushes.

At that point Tracy naturally became quite concerned. She had decided to go after her to bring her back.

"Stay here, Bonny," Tracy had shouted to her friend, "stay put; I'll go and fetch her." And as fast as she could she had started running after her.

To her dismay she learned that it isn't all that easy to catch a rebellious puppy. Zigzagging from tree to tree and bush to bush as if playing *hide and seek* with her, Tala had completely ignored Tracy's calls to come back. Fortunately, Tracy never quite lost contact with her. When she finally had caught up with Tala, her puppy was dead tired.

And so she herself was, of course!

Now Tracy still out of breath, with Tala lying at her feet, looked down on her puppy accusingly.

"Tala, I'm angry at you!" she said, wiping some perspiration off her brow, "really, really angry! Why did you run away, you stupid dog? You might have gone lost!"

It was the first time she was angry with her puppy, really angry! But after looking at her darling puppy a bit longer and remembering what she had promised her parents, her anger evaporated.

"I've no right to be angry at her," she lectured herself. "I can't blame her for what she, only a puppy! has done. What can you expect from a puppy? To stay on a trail? Rats, the only one to blame am I! I shouldn't have unleashed her. That was very stupid of me."

Tala likely understood and, of course, wholeheartedly agreed with what Tracy was thinking. To show her approval, she curled up next to Tracy and watched her with her lovely brown eyes which were almost hidden behind her floppy ears. Still out of breath, she was panting rapidly, even faster than Tracy was.

She had had the best time yet of her short life!

"Well, my dear puppy," Tracy said to Tala consolatory, "it's time for us to get back to Bonny. She must be getting quite worried by now."

Only then did she realise that she had left the leash behind with Bonny.

"How stupid can I get!" she exclaimed, "now Tala can run away a second time."

But thinking about it a little, her worry disappeared. This wasn't likely going to happen. Tala was much too tired now to run away.

Looking around, getting back to the trail wasn't such a big deal, she thought! She knew how; so it was easy. All she had to do was retrace her steps.

She, at this point was more concerned about her friend Bonny. She was hoping that she hadn't done anything unexpectedly in the meantime, as having a short nap under a tree. If she had done so, she would be sound asleep by now. Bonny, she knew, could sleep anywhere and at any time, day or night! If Bonny would be asleep, she likely would have to start searching for *her*, and finding her might be difficult. Perhaps not that difficult, Tracy though, as Bonny always snored like a pig.

The thought of perhaps finding Bonny snoring under a tree made her giggle.

Tracy got up from the dead tree branch she had been sitting on, and started to scan the wilderness to get her bearing. How exactly would she have to walk to get back on the trail? She looked around. From which direction had she come?

She closed her eyes to try to remember, but somehow that wasn't so easy. Her recollection of the chase was very patchy. She opened her eyes, and turning her head in all directions tried to spot the trail. But all she saw was the monotonous vastness of the huge wilderness around her.

It was scary!

There were few distinct features, she noticed. Groups of trees interspersed with shrubs of different kinds and shapes were all around her, but nothing looked familiar to her, nothing that reminded her of the chase - not even faintly. Just a minute ago, sitting on the tree, she had thought she could easily remember where the trail was, but now she wasn't so sure. Everything around her looked the same!

She tried to remember if she had noticed a distinct feature like a large boulder or a tall tree while chasing Tala, but couldn't. Unfortunately she had paid no attention to the surroundings.

What *did* she remember?

She did remember that at the beginning when she had started chasing Tala, she had run towards a clump of fairly tall trees where Tala was running around in circles. She also remembered that a little later she had almost tripped over a hidden branch. And she remembered too that later still, when Tala had started to zigzag, she had rested for a few minutes on a boulder. She remembered vaguely that while resting she had noted that the area around her was fairly open and grassy, with a sprinkling of a few small shrubs. When she had started running again, the terrain had become more rugged. She then had almost lost contact with Tala. When at last Tala had stopped running, completely exhausted, she finally had been able to catch up with her.

That was about all Tracy could remember.

It was quite a bit, but all much too vague to find her way back to the trail. Nervously Tracy looked at her watch, and to her amazement she noticed it was already way past noon, close to half past three in the afternoon in fact. She must have chased Tala a lot longer than she thought. Twenty minutes? Thirty? Who knows? She might even have dozed off while sitting here on the dead branch!

"And as I'll walk back to the trail instead of running," she reasoned, "it will take me at least an hour. Good grief! We'll never make it to Salmon Lake anymore today. Not likely."

She again scanned the vast wilderness around her. Suddenly a feeling that she was in trouble took hold of her. She feared that she didn't know *how* to get back! She tried to shrug it off, but couldn't. She tried to convince herself that she was worried about nothing. She grinned nervously, not wanting to admit her growing anxiety, not even to herself.

"Rats! Why *should* I be worried?" she asked herself, shrugging her shoulders. "I'm only a short distance from the trail - a few kilometres at the most. So why should I have trouble finding that stupid trail again? I'm not *that* stupid! It is easy! All I have to do is retrace my steps."

Tracy paused for a moment, and then suddenly recalled her favourite physical education teacher, Mrs. Wood, who in class always talked about her own outdoor adventures. Tracy thought:

"After I get back I'll tell her all about my adventures; and she'll giggle and joke and tell the class about it."

Tracy grinned at the prospect and ridiculed herself for thinking that finding her way back to Bonny was going to be difficult. But deep down in her heart her worry didn't subside.

Reluctantly she got up from the fallen tree.

"I better not sit on this tree any longer," she said to herself. "Like Bonny, I might fall asleep! I must get going right away. Poor Bonny will be very worried about me by now."

# Chapter 2

After she had got up from the dead tree branch, Tracy, as an eagle searching for its prey, again scanned the vast wilderness around her as carefully as possible, hoping that this time it would give her the bearing she needed to get back to the trail. But her hope was dashed. Not one familiar feature she could spot. The wilderness looked totally uninhabited and devoid of life. Not a single bird or lonely animal could be seen or heard. She was alone in the vastness. All alone.

"And now I might as well admit it," she thought. "Holy smoke! I don't know how to get back to the trail."

She was almost certain that the trail was on her left, but certain, absolutely certain she wasn't.

She walked around a little going in circles, trying to find traces of her chase - a broken branch, some flattened grass, anything at all, but could find none.

For the third time, discouraged by what she had seen, she again sat down on the tree branch to contemplate what she should do. She couldn't remain on the branch forever, of course. She *had* to take a decision. Nobody was going to take it for her. And she couldn't postpone it any longer either.

Then, dismayed, she suddenly remembered that her sense of direction had never been great. Once, when playing *hide and seek* in a field near their home with Susan, her older sister, she had become hopelessly lost as well. While she was hiding behind some bushes, her sister, failing to find her, had given up looking for her, and had suddenly gone home. Trying to get home, Tracy had walked in a totally wrong direction, lost as she was now. It had taken her almost an hour to get home. She tried to shrug off the unpleasant memory of that incident. It was too depressing.

"That can never happen to me again!" she thought. "I'm much older and wiser now."

Determined to make a plan, she got up from the branch. She was going to make a decision right away. Craning her head, she scanned the wilderness around her for the last time to make sure she hadn't missed a beacon. There was none. Then, frustrated by the lack of it, she finally decided to choose one! Her beacon was going to be a dense cluster of trees on the horizon straight ahead of her! She was going to walk straight to that beacon.

She had a very good reason for this. She remembered that on the hiking trail she had seen a lot of trees. So the trees she was seeing in the far distance very likely were those of the trail.

"If I start walking towards those trees, I definitely will get back to the trail," she said to herself, rather relieved.

It seemed sound reasoning.

Happy that finally she had a plan, she strapped her backpack on her back, and with Tala reluctantly at her side (she would have wanted to sleep a bit longer), she started walking towards the trees. But Tracy, not quite trusting her present plan, decided to take extra precautions to make her plan foolproof.

"Well," she said, looking at her watch, "I'm going to time myself how long I've walked. Let me see. If I haven't hit the trail in about an hour, I'll give up and turn around, walk back to this place, sit down on the tree again, and wait for Bonny to pick me up."

Confident that she had a second plan in place, she felt much better. Nothing could go wrong now.

Then her thoughts turned to Bonny again.

"Rats! Bonny must be quite worried about me by now," she thought. "But she shouldn't be. There's absolutely no need for that. I should be back very soon, within 60 minutes, at the most 90. And once I'm back, we'll laugh and joke about my adventures. Bonny, impressed with my survival skills, will probably tell me that I'm wonderful! That I don't need any survival course! That it would be totally wasted on me. That I perfectly know how to survive in the wilderness without."

"And I'll laugh and joke that she's right! That I can give a survival course anytime. That I'll tell my students that when you're lost, all you need is common sense and brain power. And that you should never, never panic . . ."

While turning these thoughts over in her head, she in the meantime, was making good progress towards the distant trees, and even enjoying the walk. The weather, as Master Weather had promised that morning, was perfect, and the surroundings far more pleasant to walk through than she had expected. It was open and grassy with only an occasional tree or shrub barring her way.

But that the cluster of trees she was heading for didn't seem to get much closer, started to worry her after a while. It apparently was much farther away than she had expected.

Suddenly, straight ahead, she saw a patch of flowers; the most beautiful flower she had ever seen. Deep blue they were, like the sky on a cloudless day, and almost as tall as Tracy herself. As she adored flowers, she stopped walking to look them over more closely.

But suddenly those flowers started to worry her. Why hadn't she seen them when chasing Tala? She would never have missed them had she passed through this area -flowers that large and beautiful! She hadn't been here before.

So, was she going in the right direction?

Tracy shrugged her shoulders and continued walking.

She then noticed that the vegetation around her had changed rapidly. The grass was no longer brown and pastel grey; it had changed to a much greener, more lush colour. It also was longer and tougher, hurting her ankles, making them bleed. The ground she was walking on had changed as well; it felt spongy. Just like the flowers had, the changing environment made her feel uneasy. She definitely never had gone through this type of vegetation when chasing Tala.

Was she going in the right direction?

A little later she looked at her watch. It showed that she had walked almost one hour. So according to her calculation, the trail should be very close now. She scanned the horizon trying to spot it, but saw no trace of it. She then looked at her beacon, the distant trees she was heading towards, but they seemed as far away as ever.

"Well," Tracy thought, "It's very strange! Should I turn around? No, not yet! I must be more patient."

Worried now she continued her walking through the increasingly lush and greenish vegetation.

Then something quite unexpected happened.

It happened because of Tala. Tracy hadn't seen or heard Tala for a while, and getting worried about her whereabouts, she looked back over her shoulder to see if Tala was still following her. Yes, she was, but Tala was way behind, getting very tired it seemed. Annoyed at her trailing behind that far, Tracy continued walking. But a little while later, concerned about Tala's snail's pace, Tracy looked back over her shoulder again without stopping.

She shouldn't have looked back and continued walking. The area was too soggy and muddy for that! As bad luck would have it, she suddenly stepped in a mud hole with her left foot. Her shoe sank deep into the hole, filled with water and mud, and got stuck.

Shaken by the incident, she immediately tried to pull her leg out of the hole, but couldn't. It was firmly stuck in the mud. Only after she had waited a moment and tried again, did she manage to pull it out. With a sickening *pfouff* the shoe finally broke loose. Disgusted Tracy looked down. Her leg was covered in mud almost up to her knee and her shoe filled with water.

"Holy cat! How unlucky can I get?" she shouted angrily. "Here I am, almost back on the trail, only a few minutes away from it, and now . . . and now I step in this . . . stupid mud hole . . . !"

Upset by this unpleasant incident, Tracy sat down on a boulder to decide what to do next.

"I can't possibly walk with all that water in my shoe," she said to herself. "I'll get blisters in no time! I must clean and dry my shoe before I can go on. But how?"

She thought about it for a moment. Then a broad smile appeared on her face. She could easily clean her leg and sock! It wasn't really a problem at all! She had soap in her backpack. She always took a piece along on a hike in case she needed it.

Congratulating herself on her excellent foresight, she opened her backpack, and took out the soap. But then she realised she needed more than soap for the cleaning. Frustrated, she cried:

"Rats, I need water too, clean water. Where can I find *that*?"

She thought about that for a moment, and continued:

"There must be other mud holes in the area as well. With clean water!"

She looked around and soon found one. It was just like the first one, full of water and mud. But the water on top was clean - though not quite, of course.

"It will do," Tracy told herself. "It's as clean as it ever gets here in this silly, muddy place." Then looking at the piece of soap, she said: "Now let me think. Let me plan this carefully. How should I go about it?"

She decided to first take off her shoe and sock, wash her sock with soap and water, wring it dry, then rinse her shoe in the mud hole, and then before putting on her sock and shoe again, clean her leg.

She did exactly what she had planned, and though her sock didn't get very clean (nor very dry, of course) she was rather pleased with the results.

Relieved that she had overcome this unpleasant incident more or less unscathed, she suddenly recalled with anxiety that she still had to get back to Bonny.

And soon!

"Now let me think," she said to herself, using her favourite expression again, "let me think what I should do next. Before stepping in the mud hole, I had walked about one hour towards the trees, so the trail can't be very far. I should be able to see it! So, where is that stupid trail?"

She craned her head to scan the endless wilderness for an answer. But none came. The grove of trees she had been heading for was still far, far away. If those trees stood along the trail, why weren't they much closer now?

She didn't understand that.

She looked around to see if she could spot the big boulder she had rested on when going after Tala. But though she noticed several, she didn't see the one she had sat on. Then she looked at her watch again.

Her heart skipped a beat.

The cleaning had taken over an hour!

It was much later than she had thought. The colour of the sky above the trees she was heading towards had already turned pink. The sun was slowly disappearing below the horizon. A slice of her round body had already sunk beyond the horizon. It wouldn't be long before the Lady would disappear altogether, and the Lord of Darkness again spread its black wings across the wilderness.

Fascinated at seeing the Lady disappearing in all her majesty and glory, Tracy watched as if hypnotised. Was the Lady trying to tell her something? Something she didn't know? Something she should know?

Tracy had a feeling she was!

But what could that be? Was she perhaps telling her that it was getting dark soon, and that she better find a shelter? Well, Tracy knew that, of course. That would be a silly message! She wasn't *that* stupid!

Was she perhaps telling her that the cluster of trees she had been heading for the last hour was a false beacon; that she had been walking in the wrong direction?

"Holy cow! Could that be so?"

No, Tracy didn't think so.

But a little later, being not so sure of herself anymore, she decided to think about this carefully.

She reasoned as follows:

"The sun always rises in the east and sets in the west. So for the last hour I've been walking towards the west. Is that really the right way to get back onto the trail? Let me think . . ."

She remembered from Bonny's map that morning that the trail from their campsite to Salmon Lake went north. And she also remembered that Tala had disappeared on the left side of the trail, so that was towards the west. So to get back onto the trail she must walk to the east!

Shocked by the results of her careful analysis Tracy paused. Good grief! She hadn't done that? She had walked towards the setting sun, therefore to the west.

"What? How . . . stupid can I get?" she accused herself. "I've been walking in the wrong direction! Even in the opposite direction! I have wasted two hours. And now it's getting dark."

With the sun sinking at an alarming rate now, she quickly had to decide what to do. It wouldn't be long before it was dark.

Remembering her earlier promise to go back to the fallen tree in case she couldn't find the trail, she took only a few moments to decide what to do next.

"Well," she said, "I'm going to walk straight back to that tree, and stay there for the night. And tomorrow I'm going to stay there too, and wait until either Bonny or my dad comes to pick me up. It's too risky to walk in the wilderness all by myself, not knowing where I'm going. I don't want to get *really* lost!"

That seemed a very sound plan. It meant that she just had to retrace her steps to the dead tree; she then should be very close to the trail again. Her decision made her think about her friend Bonny and her whereabouts again.

"She must be worried, that poor girl, very worried. What would she be doing now, I wonder? Looking for me off the trail? No, she would never dare to leave the trail by herself. She would be too afraid. Perhaps she has decided to wait for me under a tree, and has fallen asleep. Or perhaps she's rushing back to the motor home to tell my parents what has happened . . ."

Disturbed by all those possibilities she turned to Tala, who in the meantime had curled up under a shrub and was sleeping peacefully, totally unaware of Tracy's problems.

"Well, what do you have to say for yourself, you stupid dog?" Tracy asked her. "Yes, I know you're tired, but so am I. If you hadn't run away, we wouldn't be in trouble. I would be at Salmon Lake now, having an ice cream! Get up, Tala, we can't stay here any longer. I don't like it here! I don't want to step in another hole. We are going back to the fallen tree."

Determined, she grabbed her backpack, swung it across her shoulder, fastened the straps, and with a reluctant puppy following her from way behind, started to walk in the direction of the fallen tree.

The first kilometre was familiar and easy for her- just retracing her steps. But as it was getting darker and darker, the going became more and more difficult. Soon it had become so dark that only with difficulty could she make out where she was going. Besides, she had become very tired; she could hardly walk any more. Tracy knew that she wouldn't be able to reach the fallen tree that day any more.

She had to modify her plan - again.

She decided to try to find a shelter close by, one where she could spend the night safely.

What kind of shelter should she be looking for?

What would make a good shelter?

She sat down on a boulder to think about it. Suddenly she remembered her favourite teacher again, Mrs. Wood. Hadn't she told in class that a bunch of evergreen trees, when standing close together, makes an excellent shelter for the night when you're lost in the wilderness?

"Their thick branches keep you dry when it's raining (not, of course, when it's raining for a long time)," she had said, "and below their branches there usually is a thick layer of needles to sleep on."

Good Mrs. Wood!

Tracy's spirits lifted. She decided to follow the advice to the letter and started looking for a cluster of evergreens.

Not too far away she spotted one.

But not a friendly-looking one. In the fading twilight the trees appeared rather scary. Their black shapes with their gnarled branches looked like ghosts, telling Tracy she wouldn't be welcome at all to sleep underneath them.

But Tracy knew she had no choice. She needed a shelter, and needed it now. So she quickly overcame her fear and decided to spend the night there.

It was a very lucky decision!

When she got to the cluster, she saw it was made up of a dozen or so huge spruce trees standing very close together, as if gossiping. And beneath them - just as her teacher had so cleverly predicted, there was a thick carpet of spruce needles, inviting and smelling pleasant, cork dry.

No wonder Tracy was quite happy with her shelter. Once inside, she chose the nicest spot she could find, the one just under the thickest branch. There she took off her backpack, and with a groan of relief set down on the soft needles.

She was dead tired.

Tala followed suit. She too was dead tired. Happy with the shelter and the crunchy needles, she immediately curled up beside her, put her head down, and closed her eyes.

Tracy looked at her and felt sorry for her. Tala was still too young for all this roaming around they had done that day! She was still a baby, a puppy.

Tracy looked her shelter over, and very happy with it, wanted to share her pleasure with Tala.

She said: "Don't you think, my dear puppy, that we've got a very comfortable place for tonight? It isn't quite a 5-star hotel, but almost." And with pleasure recalling one of her dad's favourite expressions, she added,"and it's free!"

Only then did she realise how parched and ravished she was. She hadn't drunk or eaten anything since that morning! She opened her backpack, took the large water bottle she had filled at the campsite that morning, and drank and drank and drank until she couldn't drink another drop, leaving very little in the bottle.

Then she fetched the sandwiches her mom had prepared that morning. She counted four: two egg sandwiches and two peanut butter sandwiches. Eagerly she took an egg sandwich, put her teeth in it, and devoured it in no time at all. When she was about to put her teeth in the second one, she suddenly recalled (this time with annoyance) Mrs. Wood's advice about saving food in a wilderness.

"When lost in a wilderness don't eat all your food on the first day, even not if you're very hungry!" she had said. "Always save some for the following day."

"Holy cat! Had Mrs. Wood said that?"

Yes she definitely had!

And Tracy didn't like it.

"But I'm not lost in the wilderness," Tracy argued, relieved. "It doesn't really apply to me! I can't be more than an hour's walk from the trail."

Nevertheless, she decided to heed her teacher's advice, and ate only one more sandwich, the one with the peanut butter. This time eating it very slowly, taking small bites.

With lots of water and two sandwiches safely stored away in her stomach, her spirits revived. She started to feel very comfortable in her shelter; almost enjoying the adventure.

With a sigh of relief she stretched herself out on the needles, and using her backpack as a pillow, looked at the thick canopy of branches growing above her head. They looked like a frame of a large tent, she thought. They certainly would keep her safe from any rain that night.

But her contentment lasted only a short while. It was Tala's doing. She had closely watched Tracy devouring her sandwiches, and Tracy had given her nothing, not even a crust! That wasn't fair! With her brown eyes looking disapprovingly at her, moaning and barking a few times, she made it perfectly clear that she was entitled to some food and drink as well! After all, wasn't she Tracy's puppy? She should look after her properly.

Tracy noticed her, and understood, and didn't like it at all.

In fact, it irritated her.

She first decided to ignore it. With good reason! Here she was after an exhausting day, finally feeling content with life, thinking everything was under control, having saved some food for the next day as Mrs. Wood advised, and now her dog was begging for some of her precious food. She admitted that, yes her puppy had a valid point, she was entitled to some. But why did that dog not realise that she had very little, actually *nothing* to spare. Water, she definitely wasn't going to give to her. She didn't need that. That, she was quite sure of. She had had her fill at the mud holes that afternoon. But should she give her a sandwich? Half a one, perhaps?

In the end she decide to be generous, and gave her half a peanut butter sandwich. Now she had only one egg and half a peanut butter sandwich left, but that couldn't be helped. She closed her backpack, and wasn't quite sure what to do next.

She looked at her watch; it was only 8:15 p.m. - the evening was still young. Should she lie down and go to sleep right now? She looked at the inviting layer of needles below her. Sleeping on it would be quite comfortable, just as Mrs. Wood had predicted! And her pack folded up would make an excellent pillow.

It was very tempting to go to sleep right away.

She smiled at the prospect, but then decided against it. It was still way too early. Then, looking at the dry needles again, she suddenly remembered that before going on the hike that morning, she had put matches in her backpack in case Bonny wanted to brew some tea somewhere along the trail. Bonny was a real tea person. Excited she opened her backpack, and yes the matches were exactly where she had put them!

Great!

She was going to make a fire right away!

"It won't be difficult at all with all those dry needles," she remarked to herself.

With her hands she scraped together a bunch of needles and lit it with one match! Very pleased with the result she lay down, and started to enjoy it. She loved what she was seeing. It was, she thought, one of the most fascinating and relaxing campfires she had ever seen. The spruce needles made funny crackling sounds and with their blue, yellow, and purple flames they brightly lit her "cabin". With her puppy at her side and the cheerful campfire beside her, Tracy didn't feel lonely at all.

She closed her eyes, and almost immediately opened them again. She remembered she still had a little job to do. Her sock! It had never dried properly, it still was damp. Well, she was going to dry it now, above the campfire. It couldn't be easier.

She took a long stick, draped the woollen sock on one end, and with both hands held it above the flames. She had hoped that it would dry in a jiffy, but that wasn't the case. It was taking much longer. No wonder that after a while her hands were getting tired and shaky. So the stick got a bit too close to the fire, and before she noticed it, it burned a hole in her sock. A rather large hole too!

"Rats! Things never, never work out the way I've planned," Tracy cried out. "That sock was almost dry, and at the last moment I burned a big hole in it. Why do I always have such bad luck?"

She looked at her dog. Her puppy hadn't noticed anything, of course. She had curled up as close to the fire as she dared. Sound asleep, she was totally unaware of the incident. Her chest was gently going up and down, and at times she made happy noises.

"Tala is having a happy dream," Tracy thought. I wonder about what? Do dogs ever have as much bad luck as I?"

She didn't know. She didn't think so.

"Well, I'm going to lie down now" she decided. "I'm exhausted. But I don't want to fall asleep yet with the fire still going. I must keep an eye on it. I must be very careful. It might spread and get out of hand."

She took her jacket, shaped it like a pillow, and with a groan of contentment, stretched herself out on the needles.

But despite having warned herself of the dangers of an open campfire, she immediately fell asleep.

# Chapter 3

When Tracy awoke the next morning, the sun had for quite a while already shown her pink face above the horizon. Tracy hadn't noticed it as the dense canopy above her head was blocking out most of the sun rays. Still very sleepy, she wiped her eyes to see where she was; looking around she had no idea *where* she was. She looked up at the low hanging branches she had slept under, and then down on the needles she had slept on. Where was she?

Then she spotted Tala. She was curled up beside her, snoring a bit, still sound asleep. Only then all that had happened the previous day came back to her: the chase after Tala, the hole she had stepped in, the campfire, and that she was in the wilderness all by herself. She looked at the campfire and noticed it still was smouldering.

Horrified, her heart skipped a beat.

"Holy cat! How could I've been . . . so . . . darned stupid! I never put that campfire out last night," she angrily rebuked herself. "It could easily have spread and killed me and burned all the trees around me to cinders."

Upset and subdued for quite a while she murmured to herself:

"Tracy . . . Tracy you must be much, much more careful. You're all alone in the wilderness. You must look after yourself. Nobody else is looking after you!"

Then her thoughts turned to what had happened the day before.

"Yes, I made a stupid mistake to walk in the wrong direction," she admitted. "But now I know that if I walk to the east I must get back to the trail. And if I use the sun as my beacon it shouldn't be difficult at all."

Then she remembered that the previous day she had promised herself *not* to try to get back to the trail. She was going to wait at the fallen tree for Bonny or her dad to pick her up.

"True, I did promise myself that," she admitted, "but I can't possibly stay here. There's no fallen tree here. Nobody would ever find me among all those evergreen trees. No, I can't wait here. That would be stupid."

"But then . . . what shall I do?" she questioned herself.

As she was very hungry, she decided to have her breakfast before making any decision. Her stomach was crying for food!

Impatient, she opened her backpack, and noticed with dismay that she had only one egg sandwich and half a peanut butter sandwich left. She decided to eat the egg sandwich herself and to prevent another confrontation with Tala, give the rest of the peanut butter sandwich to her.

Tala had no objection to this wise decision at all! Very hungry, just like Tracy, she swallowed her allotment in one go.

But Tracy didn't give her any water.

"Tala doesn't need any," she reasoned. "On our way back we most likely will again come across some mud holes where she can have her fill. She must wait until then."

Then the time had come to get going again. She really didn't feel like walking at all. She was too tired. But knowing she couldn't stay under the spruce trees either, she forced herself to get up, and a little later she emerged from underneath the trees into the open.

The new day welcomed her with open arms. The wilderness was great for walking: soft grass all around her, and only a few shrubs and trees in the far distance. The air was pleasantly cool and refreshing, great for walking. Looking up she saw a perfectly blue sky; not a single cloud could be seen. Master Weather, it appeared, that day was in a good mood!

She decided to start walking right away, but realised she still hadn't decided where to! The time had come to make a decision! She couldn't postpone it any longer.

She sat down on a boulder to think about it.

Should she again try to find the trail she and Bonny had been hiking on, or should she try to find the fallen tree she had sat on yesterday, and wait there?

She thought about it for a moment.

It was a difficult decision to make! Yesterday, after she had discovered that she could use the sun as a beacon, she was convinced that finding the trail was easy. But now she wasn't so sure anymore. She remembered something disturbing. On the map Bonny had shown her that morning, she had seen that the trail they had been hiking on went generally to the north - but not always. There were several sharp turns both to the left and right. So, if she tried to find the trail, she might hit one of these turns, and get totally confused, thinking she was on the wrong trail.

"No," she decided, "I won't try to find that trail again. It's too risky."

But finding the fallen tree with the branch she had sat on, wasn't that easy either. She tried yesterday, and had given up.

What she needed was a better plan. A new plan.

She closed her eyes to think. Suddenly her face lit up. Yes, there was a better plan! A much better plan! Salmon Lake! She was going to walk to Salmon Lake, the lake Bonny and she wanted to go to! She clearly remembered the shape and location of the lake from the map. It was elongated, about 10 km long from east to west, about 2 km wide, and about 8 km straight north from the campsite.

"So, if it is 10 km from east to west," Tracy reasoned correctly, "and I walk to the north with the sun as my bearing, I can't miss it. And as it can't be more than a few km away from where I'm now, I will get there within a few hours. It's a very popular lake so there will be lots of boaters willing to drive me back to the campsite."

Tracy was very pleased with her brand new plan.

"It is as watertight as watertight can be," she thought.

She went over her reasoning a second time to make sure it was sound; then a third time, but couldn't find any weakness in it.

Now, Tracy felt, nothing could go wrong anymore!

"True, I don't know anything about the ground cover around the lake," she admitted. "It may be very difficult to walk through. I might have to overcome some really rough spots - dense clumps of grass and shrubs perhaps, but with some luck I easily can get to the lake."

Excited that now she had a well-reasoned plan, she turned to Tala to let her share in the good news. She was going to tell her all about it. Bending over and stroking her head, she said:

"Tala, my dear, dear puppy, I've got good news for you. We won't try to find that stupid trail any more. I shouldn't have tried yesterday either! It's too difficult. We are going to walk to Salmon Lake. That's much easier to find. It was rather stupid of me yesterday to waste all that time, don't you think? I must have been totally befuddled! If we had started walking to Salmon Lake right away, we would be back at the campsite by now!"

She laughed at the prospect.

Determined to follow her new plan to the letter, she swung her backpack on her back, and with Tala at her side happily sniffing at everything she could sniff at, and using the sun as her beacon, she started walking.

"But I must be very, very careful," she warned herself. "I should never forget that the sun isn't like a real beacon. It changes position all the time because the earth is rotating. True, the sun always rises in the east, but at noon it is in the south, and in the evening when it's setting, in the west. I should never forget that!"

As the area she was going through was perfectly flat with hardly any shrubs or dense trees to hinder her, she made very good progress.

She actually started to enjoy her walk - seeing it as a real adventure to tell Mrs. Wood about - and at times she even hummed a little song. She was delighted that now everything was under control, and going so well.

But after having walked about an hour, she noticed that the area around her had changed rapidly. The ground cover had become greener and taller than it was earlier. She even noticed some plants she hadn't seen before - moor grass and other moisture-loving plants. Tracy didn't like those changes. Uneasy now, she scanned the terrain around her more critically. Suddenly to her left she noticed a patch of large erect plants with cigar-shaped brown heads. Tracy knew them well. They were cattails.

"Cattails?" she said surprised, "I saw them yesterday as well! At the mud holes. They like to grow at really wet places, says Mrs. Wood."

She was quiet for a moment and then whispered: "What had she said? *Wet* places?"

Suddenly an eerie feeling took hold of her! This place with a patch of cattails looked very familiar!

"Am I perhaps at the same place I was yesterday?" she wondered, "the place with the mud holes?"

Upset she looked around, fearing she was.

"How stupid can I get!" she fumed. "This is crazy! Yes, this must be the same place I was at yesterday. The place with the mud holes! I must have walked in the wrong direction! But how could that be? Have I made a mistake? Again?"

She tried to assure herself she hadn't.

"No, . . . I never make a mistake twice. I'm not *that* stupid! But then, what's going on?"

Not knowing what to do next, she stopped walking.

Suddenly she had something else to worry about. Tala. She hadn't seen her for quite a while. Where was that dog? She called her, but Tala didn't show up. A moment later she spotted her a short distance away, standing behind some dense bushes.

She went over to her, and to her great surprise saw her standing in the middle of a little creek, almost up to her breast in the water, lapping it up as fast as she could.

Totally surprised Tracy shouted:

"What? A creek? Is there a creek here?"

Much relieved by her discovery she said to herself:

"See! I knew! I didn't made a mistake at all! This isn't the place of the mud holes! There was no creek there, and here there is!"

Quite relieved she looked at the creek in front of her. She loved what she was seeing. The rippling water was deep blue and crystal clear. It wasn't very deep, at the most one foot, she thought. The banks were shallow and of white sand, and numerous bushes and shrubs had found a home on them.

Then Tala heard her, and turning her head, she immediately stopped drinking. She had drunk enough of the delicious water to last her a lifetime. Swishing her tail as fast as she could, she ran towards Tracy. She then shook her wet body vigorously, and barked a few times wanting to let her know that the creek water tasted like honey.

Only then did Tracy realise how thirsty she was. Quickly she took off her shoes and socks, waded into the creek, and with both hands started to scoop up the fresh water. When she finally was satisfied, she took her water bottle, let the stale water run out, dipped it into the creek, and filled it up to the rim.

Having suddenly found such a little haven in the wilderness, Tracy couldn't resist the temptation to rest a while from her odyssey to enjoy the scenery. Salmon Lake could wait a little! It couldn't be much farther anyway.

With a smile on her face she sat down on a boulder near the creek. While admiring the beautiful green bushes along the creek, she noticed that they stood quite close together, and very close to the creek. Some of their graceful branches were so low over the creek that the tips occasionally touched the water, as if they wanted to taste it.

When Tracy saw that, she started laughing.

"Well, these bushes must love the creek. No wonder! What a beautiful place to call your home! They couldn't have found a more peaceful place than this one."

Curious about the bushes, she wondered if there would be any bird's nests in their branches.

"Most likely there will be!" she thought. "I'm going to have a look! I want to find out!"

She went to one of the tallest bushes and scanned it carefully from top to bottom. But she didn't find any nest. What she did find though, was much more exciting. Berries! The bush was loaded with berries! Purple ones, all almost as large as ripe cherries.

"Wow! Berries!" Tracy shouted.

Eagerly she tasted one, then a few more. They were as sweet as honey. She kept on eating them until there wasn't any room in her stomach left, not even for the smallest.

Stuffed, she sat down.

"This must be the luckiest day in my life!" she said to herself. "I can't believe it! A little while ago I feared I was back at the mud holes. Instead I'm at this magic creek with perfectly clean water and shrubs with berries as plentiful as the stars in the sky! It's like paradise here! I must tell Mrs. Wood all about it! She'll be quite surprised! She'll want to know where it is, and come and see for herself!"

Then Tracy, looking down at Tala who had fallen asleep at her feet, wondered if she would like the berries too. She decided to offer her some. She took a few, squeezed them with her hands until they were like a paste, and in a tempting voice said:

"Tala, Tala. Wake up! . . . I've got something for you! Berries! They're delicious! I'm sure you'll like them!"

Smiling she held her hand in front of Tala's nose.

Tala wasn't impressed. She sniffed at it a few times, then turned around, and walked away, reluctant to eat something she had never eaten before.

But Tracy didn't take *no* for an answer. Not this time! It would be excellent food for her! Tala should eat it!

"Stupid puppy, come back," Tracy cried, raising her voice, "you don't know what you're missing! Berries are very sweet and good for you! I want you to eat them!"

Tala still refused.

Tracy then took some of the paste and rubbed it on her nose. Now Tala had no choice. She couldn't possibly leave it sitting there. She had to lick it off;

like it or not. So she started licking and immediately developed a taste for it, even finishing her snack by licking Tracy's hand clean.

After her excellent lunch Tracy became very drowsy. She decided to take a little nap. She felt she had deserved it. After all, it wasn't all that late yet, and that darned Salmon Lake couldn't be that far away anyway. It could wait.

"But," she promised herself, "I will make my nap a short one, a very short one!"

Groaning with pleasure she stretched out on a grassy spot close to the creek, next to the berry shrubs. Listening to the pleasant sound of the rippling water, she closed her eyes, and as expected soon fell asleep.

Tala, never shy of an afternoon nap either, immediately followed suit. She put her head on Tracy's leg, turned over on her back, and with her legs stretched to the deep blue sky, closed her eyes as well. Apart from Tala's soft snoring and the occasional buzz of a lost fly, the wilderness around them was completely silent.

But not for long!

Suddenly, yapping from fear and without any warning, Tala jumped up. With her ears flat against her head she ran away as fast as she could, leaving Tracy behind.

Startled by Tala's strange behaviour, Tracy sat up, and saw something that paralysed her with fear. Very close to her was a huge female black bear. She was sitting on her hind legs, and staring at Tracy without making any movement. She was upset. That girl had trespassed on her territory, and what was even worse, she had stolen berries that were rightfully hers! And besides mother bear stood her cub.

Terrified, Tracy looked at the bears, not knowing what to do. She knew her life was in great danger. She knew that if mother bear would decide to kill her, she could easily do that with a slash of her paws. She had to get away from her as fast as she could.

On her hands and knees, making as little noise as possible, she crawled out from under the shrub, and started to run away faster than she had ever run before. She knew that the farther she got away from the bears the safer she would be.

But her nightmare wasn't over yet. Bad luck was following her. She suddenly heard a noise behind her. Something was running after her, trying to overtake her. Was it mother bear? Her cub? Fearing one of the bears would pull her down at any time and kill her, she tried to go faster, but couldn't.

A moment later disaster struck.

She stepped on a loose rock and fell face down on a clump of grass. She immediately tried to get up to continue running, but couldn't. She was too exhausted. In total panic now she wrapped her arms around her neck, hoping that they would protect her from the bear's sharp claws, and closed her eyes as tightly as she could . . .

Then something jumped right on top of her.

Was this the end?

Tracy groaned in terror.

But to her great surprise her pursuer hadn't been a bear. She started to lick her hands and face. Slowly Tracy opened her eyes, and to her amazement saw it was Tala! Terrified by the bears as well, she had decided that by staying close to Tracy she would be safest.

Tracy flew into a rage.

"Stupid, stupid dog! Why . . . why did you do this to me? Why did you run after me?" she shouted. "You scared me to death! I thought . . . you were one of the bears! Why didn't you bark? I would have known it was you . . ."

Tala couldn't understand a word of what Tracy was saying, of course; but from the tone of her voice she knew she had done something very wrong. To let Tracy know she was sorry and had still a lot to learn, she got down on her belly, and with her lovely brown eyes looked submissively up at Tracy.

When Tracy saw her so, she couldn't stay angry with her much longer.

"Ah well, you couldn't have known it would upset me so, Tala," she told her. "How could you? I have no right to scold you! I should be grateful. I was lucky it was only you that was chasing me. It could have been one of the bears . . ."

She stopped talking, confused by what she just had said. She thought:

"Lucky? Was I really that lucky just now?"

Coming face to face with two bears certainly wasn't lucky, she thought! But then, she could have been killed! So, had she been lucky or unlucky? She didn't know.

All mixed up now, she was quiet for a moment, and then started to cry. What just had happened was too terrible for her.

Then she suddenly stopped crying, and seeing the berry bushes in the distance, she said alarmed:

"How stupid of me! I haven't even looked if the bears have left."

With both hands shading her eyes from the sun, she carefully searched the creek area, but saw no bears. She gave a huge sigh of relief.

"Yeah! They have left!"

She sat down again, totally exhausted from the horrible encounter. She felt she couldn't go on walking anymore; she was too tired.

But above all, now too scared of the wilderness.

Tracy felt that the wilderness had suddenly turned against her! The confrontation with the bears had drastically taught her how dangerous it could be. Until now she had never thought that it could be such a frightful place, but now she knew! From now on she would be afraid of it. Behind every tree a wild animal could be lurking, and at any time a bear could be stalking her from behind.

But she knew that staying where she was, wasn't an option.

"The first thing to do now is to leave this area as soon as possible," she decided. "It's too dangerous to stay here any longer. With all those ripe berries other bears cannot be far off."

Tracy stood up and looked at her watch.

To her dismay it was way past 6 p.m. The time had passed very quickly. She realised that she wouldn't get to Salmon Lake that day any more!

"Well, in that case I might as well start looking for a shelter for the night," she reasoned.

She decided to try and find a cluster of evergreens again. The one she had slept under the previous night had been great!

"If I find one, there most likely will be a layer of needles underneath the branches," she said. "Just like yesterday. And then I can make a campfire again, and sleep on the needles with my head on my backpack, just like I did last night."

Tracy was quiet for a moment, and remembering the scary incident with the campfire the previous night, said:

"Good grief! I must be more careful than last night, much more careful! That smouldering campfire . . . it could easily have killed me!"

She scanned the terrain all around her for a cluster of evergreens, and as luck would have it, there was one. True, it wasn't very close by, nor in the direction of Salmon Lake, but Tracy didn't care; she was too exhausted to be picky. She turned to Tala to let her know of her plan, and with her dog sniffing at her side and following her closely, she started to walk quickly towards the distant evergreens.

# Chapter 4

Tracy had made an excellent choice! The evergreens she had chosen even surpassed her expectations. They turned out to be the perfect shelter for the night. There was a tiny entrance between the low-hanging branches through which she could crawl (almost like a private entrance), and inside there was a large cavity that looked like a tent. A thick layer of needles covered the ground.

Well, it wasn't *quite* a perfect haven, of course, but almost.

The branches were a little too low to the ground, and she had to remove some twigs that had fallen on the needles, and a few low-growing twigs as well, but apart from that she could find no fault with it.

"Well, what do you say my Tala ?" Tracy asked her laughingly. "Don't you like it? It's fit for a queen."

Tala agreed wholeheartedly. She loved her new shelter. She lay down right away on the soft needles, and being neither thirsty nor hungry after her creek water treat and berry lunch, quite content with the world, she fell asleep almost immediately.

Tracy took off her backpack, and as she was thirsty again from the tiring walk, decided to have a few sips of the magic creek water to celebrate her nice shelter. She opened her backpack, and rummaged through it to get her bottle. But she couldn't find it. It was a fairly large bottle, so she should have found it right away.

But she didn't.

Annoyed she turned her backpack over so that everything fell out, but none of it was a water bottle.

"Rats! Where *is* that water bottle!" she cried, irritated. "Did I *lose* it? No, I'm sure I didn't lose it! I never lose things I carry in my backpack. They can't fall out! But if I didn't lose that bottle, where the heck is it?"

Very disturbed that she couldn't find her bottle, she reluctantly put the stuff back in her pack, and tried to remember when she last had seen it.

"Holy cat! Yes. Of course! It was at the creek!"

It was there she had filled her bottle with creek water, and after she had filled it she hadn't put it back in her backpack as usual. She had left it next to her on the grass. Then she must have fallen asleep. And when Tala panicked, and she herself had started to run for her own life, she must have left it behind. That must have been the way it happened.

Bad luck *again*!

Depressed, she went over the unlucky events of the last days: the running away of her puppy, the mud hole she stepped in, the confrontation with the bears, and now the loss of her water bottle.

"One unlucky event after another! Why does it never end?" she asked herself.

She then remembered Janette Thompson, her classmate.

"Why is that girl - such an *unpleasant* girl - such a lucky girl? She's always telling lies and cheating in class and has never been caught. And she's always lucky – finding $25 on the parking lot! And she doesn't even need that money. She gets plenty from her mom. And she would never, never lose her water bottle! Oh no! Not she . . . !"

The loss of her water bottle really worried Tracy. No, she wasn't too worried about having nothing to drink that evening; she wasn't really *that* thirsty. She had had plenty to drink at the creek. But what about tomorrow? Would she stumble upon a creek again? Not likely. If not, she wouldn't have a drop of water to drink!

She tried to forget her worries by telling herself that the following day she would be at Salmon Lake anyway and be rescued, and have plenty to drink there. But she wasn't quite convinced of it. It wasn't certain at all, was it? True, in all she had walked towards the lake for several hours already, so it couldn't be *that* far any more. Of that, she was certain. But how far would *that* far still be?

Suddenly she realised that despite all the berries she had eaten, she was hungry. She knew full well there wasn't a single sandwich left in her pack - not even a tiny crumb; nevertheless she opened it, hoping that she had somehow overlooked something. Perhaps there was still a candy or piece of peppermint in a dark corner of one of the side pockets.

She slowly went through each pocket. She had gone through almost all of them when she felt something! She took it out. It was neither a candy nor a peppermint. Something much nicer!

A slab of milk chocolate.

Tracy was elated!

She loved chocolate, especially milk chocolate.

How it had got in that side pocket she didn't know. She certainly hadn't put it there herself.

"Must have been my dear Mom!" she postulated! "Yes! my dear Mom! She must have slipped it in just before we left yesterday morning, when I wasn't looking."

Impatient to taste it, she tore off some of the silver wrapping, broke a huge chunk off the slab, and started eating it. Then she ate another piece, and then another . . . and then suddenly remembered Mrs.

Wood's advice for people lost in the wilderness about saving food. Very reluctantly she decided to save the rest of the chocolate for the coming day.

With all that good stuff in her stomach, the future looked a lot brighter again! With pleasure she looked down at the carpet of needles in front of her. It reminded her of what she had promised herself a little while earlier: a campfire, and a big one! She tested a handful of the needles to find out if they were dry enough. Cork dry they were, so to get a fire going was easy. Though it wasn't quite dark yet, she was going to make it right away.

With her hands she heaped a bunch of needles together, took a match, lit some, and in no time at all she had a roaring fire going.

Pleased with the result, Tracy sat down on her folded jacket and

watched the needles burn to ashes. She loved campfires, especially those of needles. The flames jumped effortlessly from needle to needle as if chasing each other. Tracy noticed that they all had different colours: some were orange, some red, some purple, and a few even multicoloured.

That puzzled her.

"Why have the flames different colours?" she wondered. "Why aren't they all the *same*? The needles are all the same, so should therefore the flames not all be the same?"

Tracy decided to ask Mrs. Wood.

She surely would know.

Recollecting her gross negligence of the previous night, Tracy looked up to see if the flames were not getting too close to the low-hanging branches of the spruce trees. I don't want to start a fire!

None were.

"I've learned my lesson," she thought. "I'll never again forget that campfires can be very dangerous."

Watching the colourful flames and listening to the pleasant crackling of the burning needles made her very drowsy. She had the greatest trouble keeping her eyes open.

Then suddenly something startled her.

She had seen something moving on top of the needles. An intruder!

It was a mouse!

It happened so fast that she wasn't quite sure she had *really* seen him. She sat up to see better and looked again. Yes, it was a mouse! A fat mouse had emerged from underneath the needles, only a few feet from where she was. He was still there, motionlessly looking at her with his tiny eyes, probably wondering what kind of an intruder she was.

Tracy cried out in terror. Scared of the noise, the mouse ran away as quickly as he could. But he didn't get very far. Tracy hadn't been the only one who spotted him; Tala had too. Jumping up, she ran after him, and caught him.

Scared stiff, Tracy watched what happened next.

Tala, proud of having caught the intruder, with him in her mouth, came to her to show her her catch. Tracy saw that the mouse was still alive; his long tail was wiggling as a leaf in a breeze. Then Tala curled up next to her and started to eat him.

"Good grief!," Tracy moaned! "Who . . . who would have thought that the needles I'm sitting on and was going to sleep on, harbour mice? And that my dear puppy kills them and eats them? She, my own dear Tala!"

Tracy was silent for a moment. Then, trying to justify the outrageous behaviour of her puppy, she said:

"She must be very hungry, poor thing, otherwise she would never, never have done it! But if - oh my gosh! - if she is still hungry after eating this mouse, she may go and look for another one. Finding them won't be difficult at all. Lots of them most likely live under these needles. They never live by themselves."

"Yak! What in heaven's sake am I going to do?" she asked herself. "I can't possibly sleep on those needles tonight. I will be sleeping on top of the those terrible creatures! They may be curious, and crawl all over me when I'm asleep."

Tracy was close to crying. She looked at her smouldering campfire for an answer, but none came. The dancing flames looked awful now, like mice wiggling their tails.

After a little while though, Tracy started to calm down and pondered what she should do. Should she leave the shelter and try to find another one?

"Actually," she thought, "actually, I shouldn't do anything. Nothing at all! It's quite ridiculous to be scared of those little animals. Haven't I seen much bigger ones! Were the bears I saw this afternoon not a thousand times bigger and a million times more dangerous than this little mouse? So why should I be afraid of these creatures? They won't bite and they won't scratch. In fact, Josin (one of her class mates) even keeps them as pets. She says they are very friendly creatures. They like to sit on her hands, and nibble on her fingers."

But all her reasoning didn't make her fear of them disappear. She knew it was ridiculous, yet for the life of her she wasn't going to sleep on those needles that night.

Suddenly she smiled.

She had found a perfect solution.

"Ah! That's it! How stupid of me! Why for heaven's sake haven't I thought of that earlier? Tala is the solution! I'm going to sleep with Tala beside me. Not a single mouse, not even the most pesky one would dare to come near me. If he does, it will be his last adventure with an awful ending: Tala will eat him!"

Happy with the solution, she immediately implemented her plan. Carefully she extinguished the fire, and with her dear puppy curled up tightly against her, she soon forgot all about the mice that might have been crawling underneath the needles, and fell asleep.

# Chapter 5

The next morning when Tracy opened her eyes, she was totally confused and bewildered. She didn't know *where* she was. All she knew was that she was very, very hungry and very, very thirsty. Seeing her backpack, without giving it any thought she grabbed it, opened it, and started searching for her water bottle and sandwiches. But, of course, she couldn't find anything. Then it slowly dawned on her where she was, and she remembered all that had happened.

She hadn't a crumb to eat or a drop to drink.

She had left her water bottle at the creek, and yesterday she and Tala had eaten the last of the sandwiches.

Frustrated, she threw her pack down.

She then, in a very bad mood, turned to Tala. She was still sound asleep, snoring softly, thinking she was back in the motor home perhaps - totally oblivious of Tracy's troubles.

Tracy thought:

"And it all is her doing! She's the cause of all my troubles!"

Angry at Tala, raising her voice, she said:

"Hey there! You stupid dog! If you hadn't run away I wouldn't be so hungry and thirsty now. I wouldn't be here in this wilderness. And you Tala, you probably don't care a darn *where* we are. And while I'm starving, you probably aren't even hungry after eating that fat mouse yesterday evening; and won't be hungry for a long time with that thing in your stomach."

Her speech hadn't woken Tala up yet.

Shouting as loud as she could now, she said:

"Rats! It's . . . not . . . fair!"

That did it! It woke Tala up!

Tala strongly disliked the manner in which she had been woken up! She wasn't used to that! What was the matter with Tracy? Why was she so upset with her? She got up and tried to lick Tracy's hand to calm her down, but looking at her face, she realised that *this* time she wouldn't be receptive to any expression of her love.

So she didn't.

Confused, she turned away.

Tracy, who had been watching Tala, suddenly was ashamed of herself.

"My goodness!" she thought. "Shouldn't I be grateful for what my puppy has done? If she hadn't slept next to me last night, I would have been dead scared, and not slept a wink. I shouldn't have scolded her so."

So she said in a conciliatory tone:

"I'm sorry Tala! I - I shouldn't be angry with you! Of course, it's not your fault that things have gone wrong. It's all my fault, really. I should never have unleashed you. I should have known better and . . . ."

Not knowing what to say next to her puppy, she paused.

"Well," she continued after a little thought, "as there's nothing to eat nor to drink for either of us, we might as well get going, don't you think, Tala?"

She took her pack, swung it across her shoulder, but then suddenly remembered the slab of chocolate in the side pocket. She quickly put down her pack again, took the chocolate, broke off four pieces, and started to eat them, giving nothing to Tala.

But she couldn't hide her treasure from Tala. Of course not! With her brown eyes she had seen everything that Tracy was doing, hoping to get some of the chocolate as well.

A bit rattled, Tracy looked at her. She didn't quite know what to do. Should she give her some of her chocolate? Did she really need it? Would she like it?

No! She didn't need it, Tala decided. Not at all. She had eaten a whole mouse last evening. So, she couldn't be hungry at all. Besides, she probably wouldn't like chocolate anyway.

But still feeling ashamed for scolding her without any reason a minute ago, she changed her mind. Grudgingly she broke off a few pieces and gave them to Tala. She, not very particular about what she ate as long as it was edible, swallowed the chocolate without any objection.

Then it was time to leave the shelter. Reluctantly Tracy put her backpack back on her shoulders. But immediately she was tempted to take it off again and go back to sleep. She was too tired to walk another hour, let alone another day. It was very tempting to stay under the evergreens and go back to sleep!

She thought about it for a moment.

"My dad certainly will be looking for me by now, and find me here," she reasoned, trying to come up with a good reason to go back to sleep. But she knew full well that nobody would ever find her here, deep under the evergreens.

So a little later she forced herself to get going, left the grove and started walking towards Salmon Lake with the sun as her bearing. The terrain ahead wasn't as smooth and inviting as it had been the previous day. It was covered with lots of bushes, boulders and weeds, making walking difficult. She often had to go around the obstacles, and that slowed down her walk to a snail's pace.

Looking at the sky after an hour or so of walking, she noticed that the weather was changing. True, the sun was still showing her smiling face, and the air was still nice and warm, but in the west, above some distant trees, ominous changes were happening. Ugly black clouds were popping up from nowhere, promising big trouble.

Master Weather, probably in a bad mood, was brewing up something nasty!

For quite a while she decided to ignore the threatening and increasing cloud formations behind her, hoping that if she would, they somehow would magically go away.

But they didn't!

The clouds became darker and darker, and larger and larger.

Soon the sun disappeared behind one of the clouds, and the temperature fell rapidly. Tracy, finally turning her head, scanned the sky behind her again.

It was alarming!

Instead of the few isolated towering clouds she had seen a little while ago, there now were many, bigger and darker than before; some even right above her head. The sun was totally hidden, and there was only one patch of blue sky left.

Tracy couldn't ignore the threatening weather any longer.

"It's going to rain," she said to herself. "And a lot too! And it will start very soon! I better find some shelter before it is too late."

Turning to her puppy, she said:

"Quick Tala! We must find some evergreens. It's going to pour! I don't want to get soaked!"

She quickly scanned the area around her, and saw some tall bushes towards the east, but no evergreens except in the far distance towards Salmon Lake.

Turning to Tala again she said:

"We're out of luck Tala, there isn't any shelter close by. We might as well keep on walking and hope for the best."

But the best never came.

Without any warning at all, it started to pour. In buckets without a break the rain fell down on her. Tracy quickly tried to get her rain coat out of her backpack, but in her haste she had trouble opening the zipper. By the time she finally had opened her pack and taken her jacket out, she was soaked. Not only her clothing, but also most of the items in her backpack.

Then, without warning, Master Weather, being in a particularly bad mood that day, made the day pitch dark and then started thundering and lightning as loud and blinding as he could. Through the black sky he threw down lightning flashes every few seconds that looked like furious snakes. Each one was accompanied by a deafening thunderbolt. Some of the lightning landed so close to where she was that she feared she would be hit at any moment. She didn't know what scared her the most: the rain, the thunder or the blinding lightning! Never before had Tracy been in weather as terrifying as this.

Hoping that the long grass she stood on somehow would protect her from the fury of Master Weather, Tracy fell down on her knees and hid her face in the grass. Then she wrapped her arms tightly around her neck and closing her eyes, expected the worst.

But the thunderstorm, like most, didn't last very long. The flashes and the sickening thunderbolts became less and less frequent. And then the dark sky opened up, and Master Weather, his fury spent, let the sun show her friendly face again.

It was as if the ordeal had never happened.

Dazed, Tracy finally dared to open her eyes and slowly got up. She looked around. The downpour had flattened most of the vegetation, ripped off many leaves, and had turned the grass around her into a mud pool. She looked at her clothes. From her head down to her feet she was covered in mud. She looked like a slimy creature that makes its home in deep dark caves.

Only then did she wonder what had become of Tala. Where was she? Tracy didn't see her. She hadn't heard her bark during the thunderstorm either.

But she wasn't far off. Tracy spotted her only a few feet away. She was also soaking wet, but to her great surprise not muddy at all!

And not wet much longer either.

As Tracy was watching her, Tala with a few powerful shakes of her body, got rid of most of the water, and within no time at all, was dry, looking as if she had never been in the violent thunderstorm at all. Rather thirsty after all the excitement she ran away, and started licking up some of the water from a puddle.

"Good grief!" Tracy exclaimed. "How can that be? That terrible thunderstorm didn't even touch her! How can she be that clean? She must have found a much better shelter than I did. And now she is quenching her thirst while for me there's nothing to drink except muddy water!"

"That dog . . . ! She has all the luck in the world!"

Watching Tala drink, Tracy quickly realised that she had been wrong to envy her. There was enough water for her to drink too. Dripping bushes! Granted, what was dripping off the leaves wasn't quite clean, but reasonably clean it was!

But she better hurry! They wouldn't be dripping for long!

She looked around, and spotted several bushes with water still dripping from their large leaves. She quickly crawled under a bush, turned over on her back, opened her mouth, and let the water run right into her mouth.

Like Tala, she soon had quenched her thirst as well.

Hungry now she decided to eat something. With great pleasure she remembered the chocolate in her backpack. She was going to have some. She opened her backpack, and to her great disappointment saw that almost everything inside was soaking wet, including her precious chocolate. Grimacing in disgust, she fished it out. It was sticky and gooey. Her first reaction was to throw it away, but she quickly changed her mind.

"That would have been very stupid!" she rebuked herself. "I can easily make it edible again. I'm going to put it in the sun on a rock to dry. It soon will be fine again!"

After she had done that, she sat down on a boulder, still sopping wet, and as the sun had disappeared again behind a towering cloud, she started to shiver from the cold. She wondered what she should do after the chocolate had dried. Very likely her clothes wouldn't then be dry yet.

"I'll stay here until my clothes are dry too," she said decisively. "I can't possibly walk in wet clothes. I would get sick. I can't do anything about the mud, but that can't be helped."

Dismayed with having so much bad luck that day, she said:

"This is another unlucky day for me! Will my bad luck never stop?"

Closing her eyes, slowly getting warm and comfortable as the sun had appeared again, she dozed off. But a grave mistake it was! She should have been more careful. When a little while later she opened her eyes and looked at the rock with the chocolate on it, she saw something very upsetting.

Tala was there.

She was eating her chocolate!

As fast as she could Tracy jumped up and ran to her puppy, trying to salvage some of her precious chocolate! But it was too late. When she got to the rock all that was left was a tiny piece that had accidentally fallen in the mud and some sticky chocolate wrapping flapping in the wind.

Furiously stamping her foot on the grass as hard as she could Tracy turned to Tala, and shouted:

"Stupid dog! That chocolate wasn't for you! I never told you you could have it! Go away!"

Disgusted with Tala she sat down again. Everything that day had gone wrong: a thunderstorm, getting soaked, and now her chocolate eaten by Tala - one stroke of bad luck after the other.

Enviously she looked at Tala and thought:

That dog! Why was she such a lucky dog? Since running away she had had one stroke of luck after the other: plenty to drink each day, a mouse for supper last night, and now chocolate for lunch.

"That . . . was . . . not . . . fair!"

Still wet, Tracy started to shiver uncontrollably. The sun had disappeared again, this time behind a cumulus cloud that didn't want to go away. She touched her clothes, and though no longer wet, they still were damp.

"Well, as the sun can't make up her mind and keeps on disappearing, I might as well start walking in my wet clothes," she thought. "Salmon Lake can't be that far any more!"

But that, she knew, she had been telling herself for the last two days many times over. And she hadn't seen a glimpse of that stupid lake yet!

Why was it taking so long? Where was it? Had it disappeared?

Then suddenly horrible thoughts came up in her mind. Maybe she *still* was going in the wrong direction . . . Maybe she had been wrong again . . . All the time . . . Maybe the sun in a wilderness wasn't such a reliable beacon after all . . . Maybe the lake was still a long, long way away, 20 km perhaps, who knows . . . May be 500 km . . . Maybe she would never find it . . . May be she . . .

Groaning from despair, she stopped dead in her tracks. She tried to dispel these horrible thoughts from her mind, but that wasn't so easy! Like rain showers they kept on coming back and back. Then she suddenly recalled what her mom had often said to her:

"Tracy, fear nothing except fear itself."

These words gave Tracy the strength to start going again.

With her wet backpack on her shoulders, and Tala at her side, she started walking again. She looked at the sun, and remembered that now, late in the afternoon, to get to the lake, she should walk away from the sun, even keeping it a bit to her right.

For quite a while she made good progress. The terrain was reasonably flat, and though she had to avoid a few dense patches that were blocking her way, she could keep on going in the right direction.

Then gradually the terrain became so rough that her progress turned into a snail's pace. High boulders were blocking her way everywhere, and far more tenuous bushes than she had met anywhere on her odyssey, were holding her back. At places they stood so close together that she doubted she would ever find a way through.

Tracy tried to keep going, but after a little while she gave up. She simply was too exhausted to go on. Dead tired, she decided to start looking for a shelter for the night.

"Finding a good shelter of evergreens shouldn't be difficult at all," she thought. "I found one yesterday and one the day before, so there's no reason why I shouldn't find one now. All I need is a few tall evergreens clustered together, with lots of dry needles underneath. Ah! . . . and then I'm going to make a huge fire to dry my clothes, and then I'm going to sleep on the needles using my backpack as a pillow again and tell Tala to curl up tightly against me to protect me from mice again! With her at my side I won't be afraid of anything, not even an army of mice!"

With all these exciting things planned, she immediately started to scan the wilderness for evergreens. But she saw none. There were plenty of trees, but all had leaves, not needles. True, many of the trees she saw grew in dense clusters too, like the evergreens, and they likely had a thick layer of leaves underneath their branches as well. But Tracy didn't want leaves for her campfire nor for her mattress. For both she wanted needles! She was absolutely sure that needles make much better campfires and are far more comfortable to sleep on.

Hoping that she had not looked properly, she scanned the area again for evergreens, but there were none. She then gave up looking. She was so tired and cold that she decided to seek shelter under the trees with leaves after all.

"And why shouldn't I?" she questioned herself a minute later. "What do I *really* know about sleeping on leaves? Nothing at all! I've never slept on them. Perhaps they are much more comfortable than evergreen needles. Who knows? Perhaps leaves make better campfires too! Who knows? And I'm positive there won't be any mice under leaves. They don't like leaves. At least, I've never heard they do."

With all that positive thinking going on in her mind, Tracy actually started to look forward to spending the night under deciduous trees. She headed straight for the closest stand.

But as she had feared, the trees weren't as good a shelter as the evergreens had been. They stood rather loosely together so that there wasn't a cosy entrance as had been beneath the evergreens. And their branches didn't make a cosy tent-like canopy either. They were awful!

But on the positive side, yes, there *were* plenty of leaves underneath the trees. They smelled nice too, and were cork dry.

Still shivering from the cold, she decided to make a campfire right away. A roaring one. Just the thought of it made her feel warm. She took off her pack, got on her knees, and with her hands heaped together a bunch of leaves. Quite a lot she needed as the evening was still long.

Then she went to her pack and fetched the matches. She opened the box, and to her dismay saw that they looked rather strange; there was something wrong with them. The tips had smudged the inside edge of the box red!

"Oh darn, darn it." she cried loudly, using the strongest phrase she ever used. "They're wet! Now I can't make a campfire. I can't dry my clothes either. What shall I do now?"

Devastated she lay down on the leaves and closed her eyes. She started to cry. The situation had become desperate. She knew that if she couldn't make a fire, she likely would get sick, would catch a really bad cold, even pneumonia.

All that time Tala had been watching her. Did she understand what was going on? That this was the time Tracy really needed her, needed her desperately?

Yes Tala did!

Slowly she walked over to Tracy, looked searchingly at her with her brown eyes, and putting her legs on her shoulders, she curled up beside her as closely as she could. She was going to make sure Tracy would stay warm that night!

Delighted, Tracy wrapped her arm around Tala. Her warm body immediately warmed hers. With Tala beside her, Tracy felt as if she was close to a nice campfire after all. A super one. One she didn't have to put out, one she could enjoy all night without fear of endangering herself.

"Oh Tala," she whispered. "Thank you . . . for coming beside me . . . For . . . keeping me warm tonight . . . Sorry about . . . about the chocolate . . . I lost my temper . . . It wasn't your fault at all . . . ! I . . . shouldn't have put it on that rock . . . I shouldn't have . . . "

A few minutes later she was asleep.

# Chapter 6

When Tracy woke up the next morning, it was still very early. Even the sun, always an early riser, hadn't risen yet. She tried to stand up, but couldn't. She was too disoriented. She had a nauseating headache, and her throat was terribly swollen.

Tracy had slept very poorly that night. Mind you, it wasn't Tala's fault! Throughout the night she had kept Tracy nice and warm, and she hadn't left her, not even once. The real reason why Tracy had slept so poorly was that she had had terrible dreams. About scary creatures like spiders, centipedes and black snakes. She had dreamed that they were crawling all over her body and getting in her hair. She had tried to shake them off, but they wouldn't go away.

Her belief that needles are nicer to sleep on than leaves was proved right. All night long, she had tossed and turned from side to side to find a comfortable sleeping position, but had found none.

Now Tracy tried to stand up again. Holding fast onto a tree branch, she finally succeeded. She then decided to talk to Tala. She wanted to let her know that she was sick. Really sick. That she wasn't going to walk any more. But when she tried, Tala couldn't make head nor tail of her words. They were like groans, totally incomprehensible.

A little later Tracy tried to communicate with Tala once again, but failing again, she gave up. Disgusted, not realising what she was doing, she took her backpack and opened it, hoping to find some scraps of food.

"But why should I do such a stupid thing, open my pack and look for food?" she questioned herself angrily. "I should know by now it's empty! Quite, quite empty! I haven't got a crumb of bread to eat nor a drop of water to drink."

She was quiet for a moment, threw down her backpack and continued:

"But I don't care . . . Why should I care? I'm not hungry at all. I don't *want* food. I want to sleep. All I want is sleep."

A little later she found herself lying on the leaves again, half awake. She couldn't remember how she had got there. Had she become so dizzy that she had fallen down? She couldn't remember.

She started to talk to herself, babbling like a small child, not knowing what she was saying:

"Why . . . why aren't they looking for me . . . ? Does nobody care . . .? Where is Bonny . . . ? My dad should be looking for me . . . With a plane . . . . Where is he . . . ? Why doesn't he come . . . ? I don't want to walk anymore . . . I'm going to stay here . . . ."

She was quiet for a moment. Stay here? She couldn't possibly stay here. She continued:

"But . . . if I stay here . . . under the trees asleep on the leaves, they'll never find me. I must get up and go to Salmon Lake. There are lots of boats there . . . and people."

Soon after, with Tala at her side, she found herself as if in a bad dream outside the trees, walking in the open air. Her legs were quite wobbly, unwilling to carry her, and her head was throbbing as if there were needles inside. Disoriented, she straggled along, most of the time unaware of where she was going.

A little later she suddenly stopped in her tracks. Bewildered, she looked at herself and the endless hostile wilderness around her:

"Rats! Where am I? Where am I going? Am I going in the right direction? I should be going to Salmon Lake! Where is the sun? It should be on my right. Is it? Let me see . . . "

She looked up at the sky, but the sun wasn't on her right!

It was behind her.

"How stupid can I get," she rebuked herself sharply, "going in the wrong direction! Why am I not using the sun as my bearing?"

She quickly started walking in the right direction.

After Tracy had struggled through the wilderness for about an hour, she lifted up her throbbing head and saw a large stand of trees on the horizon. They were tall and stood very close together. They almost looked like a edge of a forest. None of the trees were evergreens.

"If they aren't evergreens what kind of trees are they?" questioned Tracy. "Of course! Now I know. If they have leaves they must be deciduous trees."

Tracy was very discouraged by what she saw, wondering if she would ever be able to walk through them.

A while later Tracy finally recognised them. They were poplars. "Why are there so many in the same area?" Tracy wondered. "What can be the reason?"

She didn't know the answer and wished she could ask Mrs. Wood. Thinking about it a little longer her face lit up, and she started to smile. Of course, she knew the answer! She remembered! When explaining the different types of trees growing in the wilderness Mrs. Wood had said that you often find poplars around lakes because they're water-loving.

"So the trees I'm seeing on the horizon must be the poplar trees of Salmon Lake," Tracy concluded.

There was no other explanation.

Tracy was jubilant! A huge burden had been taken off her shoulders. She finally knew for sure she was getting very close to Salmon Lake. In her excitement she turned to Tala. She wanted to share the good news with her puppy.

"Oh Tala," she said, getting on her knees and stroking her head. "Tala, I've got news. Very good news my dear, dear puppy!"

And pointing her finger to the distant trees, she said:

"Look, Tala! Those trees over there! Those tall ones? Those are poplars. Those are trees growing around Salmon Lake! Our odyssey is nearly over! And when we get to the lake there will be lots of boats with friendly boaters to pick us up and . . . "

Suddenly she stopped talking.

What? Pick her and Tala up in their boat?

She critically looked at herself, then at Tala, and then at herself again.

"But . . . would . . . would the boaters be *willing* to pick us up? A girl all covered in mud, with a big hole in her sock, with a smelly dog?"

Her expectation of soon going to be rescued turned sour.

Nobody was going to pick her up. She looked like a tramp and hadn't showered for days! Who would want to take a girl like she with her dirty dog in their clean boat?

Nobody!

"Ah! Don't worry about it, Tracy," she continued her monologue trying to convince herself that there was no reason to worry. "Even if some of the boaters refuse to pick us up, there always will be others - passionate people - who will. Especially when they hear that for four days we have had nothing to eat or drink and are starving."

Nothing to eat or drink? Starving?

That wasn't quite true, of course! Critically she looked at Tala.

Tala wasn't starving at all! She had eaten all kind of things on their odyssey: a mouse, sandwiches, and her chocolate. And she showed it. Tala was still running around as if her owner had taken her for an afternoon walk, indifferent to all the troubles *she* was having.

It suddenly irritated Tracy to see Tala in such good shape.

That . . . wasn't fair!

"Are dogs always that lucky?" she asked herself. "Why? Or are they just more clever than people?"

Tracy didn't know.

Deep in thought about that question, Tracy continued her journey towards Salmon Lake.

As the morning wore on, it was getting warmer and warmer. There wasn't a cloud in the sky, and the sun with her rays was shining relentlessly down on them. The vegetation had become far more troublesome too. The grass was about a foot high and the sharp blades often wrapped around her legs, causing them to bleed. The shrubs in places were so close together and intertwined that they formed an almost impenetrable barrier. But what kept her going were the distant poplars. They were getting closer and closer!

A little while later, at midday, Tracy had become so tired that she couldn't continue any longer. She needed a place to rest, a shady one. And as quickly as possible. She soon found one. It was a lovely mossy spot in the shade of some large trees. Exhausted, she threw down her pack, stretched out on the cool moss, closed her eyes, and almost immediately was sound asleep.

But not for long.

A clump of moss landed on her face. Startled, Tracy set up, and looked around to see where it had come from. It came from Tala! She stood a little distance away from her, and with her front legs was frantically digging in the soft moss. Clumps of moss were flying high up into the air, and one almost landed right on Tracy's body.

She was just about to reprimand Tala sternly for her outrageous behaviour, when to her amazement Tracy noticed that Tala had put her nose in the hole and started licking at the moss.

Now Tracy became very curious.

"Licking at moss? Why is she licking at moss? Does she like that? I thought dogs don't."

Tracy then decided to leave Tala alone and lay down on the moss again. It was at that point that she noticed that part of her clothing was wet, the part she had lain on.

"What? My pants wet? How can that be? Wait! Then the moss must be wet!"

Then the strange behaviour of Tala became crystal clear to Tracy. She was thirsty and was licking at the moss because it was wet!

"Wow! How clever!"

Very thirsty herself, forgetting that the water in the moss might be rather muddy - poisonous perhaps - she immediately followed Tala's lead. Getting on her knees she started digging up the moss and squeezing it out. To her great delight, in no time at all, enough had dripped out to quench her thirst. Never in her life had soggy mossy water tasted so good.

Her thirst quenched and having slept a little, she felt much better. But now suddenly she was hungry. She wanted food. Looking around she hoped she could find something edible here as well, like berries. But that was highly unlikely, she thought. Nevertheless, she started looking in the bushes nearby, but found none.

"Perhaps the moss itself is edible," she thought. "I'm going to try it!"

She put some in her mouth but spat it out almost immediately. It tasted terrible.

Then suddenly something of interest caught her eyes. A few feet away, just behind the moss patch, she noticed a plant that didn't look like moss at all.

"What is it?" she thought. "Perhaps it's edible"

Curious, she decided to have a closer look.

She went over to the mysterious plant, and carefully inspected it. It was round, white, had no leaves, and was fairly large, almost the size of her hand. She couldn't identify it, but remembered having seen it somewhere before. But for the life of her, she couldn't recall where, and when. Then she noticed a few more of them- smaller and larger ones - and except their size, they all looked similar.

Then suddenly she remembered.

She said:

"Aha! Of course! Of course I know what they are! They are mushrooms. The ones Mom sometimes buys. I've eaten them in my salad. They're delicious!"

Tracy was delighted!

"Lucky me!" she cried. "Mushrooms! I've found mushrooms!"

Master Fate, likely in a good mood that day, had decided to take an immense load off her shoulders. She felt a thousand pounds lighter! She was going to eat them all. Stuff herself!

Smiling broadly, she picked one of the largest mushrooms she could find. But as she was about to put it in her mouth, a scary thought entered her mind:

"Aren't many mushrooms poisonous? Rats! Perhaps the one I'm about to eat is poisonous as well!"

She knew from Mrs. Wood that you must be very, very careful with mushrooms. "Some are so dangerous," she had told in class, "that a tiny sliver can kill you in seconds. And only an expert can tell the difference between poisonous and non-poisonous ones."

Her joy of finding mushrooms evaporated.

"Now what? What shall I do now?" she cried.

True, the mushroom in her hand looked like the ones she had eaten at home - the non-poisonous ones - but was this one the same? *Exactly* the same? Fixated she stared at it. No, it wasn't the same. It was much *larger* than the ones she had eaten at home, about twice their size.

"Twice as large . . . But does that matter? Does size make mushrooms poisonous?"

Very carefully now, like a professional botanist, she inspected the mushroom in her hand further to see if she could detect more differences from the ones she had eaten at home.

To her horror there were!

The mushroom had tiny red spots, right in the middle. Not many, mind you - eight at the most - and hardly visible, but red spots there definitely were.

Tracy now dead scared, dropped it as if it was a scorpion!

Devastated, she cried out:.

"How unlucky am I! . . . Here I find mushrooms . . . lots of them . . . and I'm starving; and I can't eat them because they might, only *might* be poisonous! . . . Oh! What shall I do?"

She thought about it for a moment and said:

"Perhaps I should eat a tiny sliver and see what happens."

She was dead quiet for a moment and then whispered:

"See what happens? But if it is poisonous, it will kill me. I may die a horrible death, or get a stomach ache so terrible that I cry out in pain for hours, perhaps days; and nobody will hear me here in this horrible wilderness. And in the end I will die alone, all alone . . ."

That horrible prospect settled it!

"No," she decided, "I'm not going to eat that mushroom. I've had too much bad luck so far. No, it's too dangerous. I'm not going to touch it. It may kill me!"

Suddenly her face cleared up. She had found a solution! A good one too.

Tala!

She was going to offer Tala a piece of the mushroom. She was going to use Tala as a guinea pig! If Tala wouldn't die within a few minutes, the mushroom wouldn't be poisonous and she could eat them.

Slowly, deep in thought, somewhat happy but not overly happy with her dubious plan, she reluctantly picked up the mushroom she had dropped, and broke off a small piece with a few red spots on it.

She quietly looked at the awful spots.

And then at Tala . . .

"But . . ." she softly said to herself, "but if it is poisonous I'll poison my own puppy! She will die! I would have killed her! It would be my doing!"

She winced . . . She didn't know *what* to do.

It was an agonising decision to make for a 14-year old girl! For quite a while she stood there deep in thought, as if frozen. She then dropped the mushroom, and squashed it under her shoe.

"It would have been such a cruel betrayal of trust," she whispered. "If Tala would have died, I'd never have forgiven myself!"

Totally drained from this nerve-wrecking experience, she wanted to lie down on the cool moss again, close her eyes, and sleep until the next day or the day thereafter. She felt she couldn't walk any more, not a single step. But deep down in her heart she knew she had to go on; she had no choice!

With great difficulty, with Tala coming along unwillingly as she wanted to sleep as well, Tracy started walking again. She knew for certain she was very, very close to the lake now. The many poplar trees, the dense shrubs, the moist moss, the mushrooms - all that pointed to the fact that Salmon Lake was just around the corner!

But as she got closer and closer to the lake, the shrubs and bushes stood so close together that finding a way through them was almost impossible. It was like trying to walk through a tropical jungle. She wondered if she would ever make it to the lake.

But suddenly the tiny track she was on widened. It became almost twice as wide, almost like a real trail. At first she didn't dare to believe what was happening, expecting the trail to narrow again around the next corner and turn into a jungle of weeds and branches again. But that didn't happen. The track actually got wider and wider.

It finally became a real trail!

Her lucky star hadn't left her after all!

Suddenly she saw something that made her cry out from joy! Footprints! Footprints on the trail - small ones and large ones. The small ones were likely from a child's shoe; the larger ones from a man's boot.

People had recently walked on the trail!

Immensely relieved that anytime soon she would see the lake, she started walking as fast as she could.

"It won't be more than a few minutes to get to the lake now," she said excitedly, "five at the most. And there will be lots of boaters to rescue me. And they'll give me sandwiches. Peanut butter and ham sandwiches and much more, and then . . ."

She was so lost in her thoughts and projections that she didn't see it.

It was a wasp nest.

It hung from a branch right in the middle of the trail. Not easy to see, though. But if Tracy had been more observant she would have.

Then a terrible thing happened.

She bumped her head right against it.

Fortunately she didn't do much damage to the nest – she just displaced it a bit. Nevertheless, the wasps were terribly upset. They didn't want any bumping on their treasure. As going to war, thinking that she *on purpose* had done it, hundreds of angry wasps swooped down on her, trying to punish her for what she had done.

For a split second Tracy had no idea what was happening to her. She stood there as if frozen. But then, seeing the angry wasps buzzing around her and feeling their terrible stings, she knew. She was in deep trouble. She ran away as fast as she could, chased by the stinging wasps. She managed to get quite a distance from the nest, but then another disaster struck! She tripped over a dead tree branch that was hidden under some grass, and fell flat on her face right in a muddy puddle.

Deadly afraid of the swarming wasps she tried to get back on her feet, but couldn't. The fall had badly hurt her ankle. She had strained it! Desperate to protect her body from the aggressive wasps as much as possible, she started to scoop up the mud from the puddle with both hands, and spread it on her body.

She did the right thing!

The soft mud immediate formed a protective layer on her body, stopping the wasps from stinging her any further. It also soothed the excruciating pain of the many stings. Soon most of them had left. A few pesky ones kept on circling around her, but as they couldn't sting her any more, they soon left as well.

For quite a while, more dead than alive, in great pain, Tracy lay there in the wet mud, without moving. When she finally opened her eyes and tried to get on her feet, it was getting dark. The sun, tired of shining all day, had started to disappear. It had already painted the tree tops red and put long shadows across the trail, warning Tracy that it would be dark soon.

Scared of having to sleep another night in the wilderness, she finally sat up and managed to get on her feet. She tried to walk. But she couldn't. Her right leg, badly sprained from the fall, failed to support her.

Then she suddenly remembered Tala. Where was she? Had Tala been stung as well? Tracy turned her head and looked around. She spotted Tala almost next to her, lying on her back, in great pain as well, licking herself wherever she could. She too had been badly stung. Tracy wanted to tell Tala that she was going to put some mud on her body as well, but her words were like groans, totally incomprehensible. She couldn't talk any more. Her whole face had swollen up from the stings.

A frightening thought now flashed through her head:

"Wasps stings? Am I going to die?"

Wasn't it Mrs. Wood who had said that when you have been stung by a wasp, even only once, you should see a doctor immediately? If you don't and happen to be allergic, you may die within hours! And she hadn't been stung only once, but many times over!

Was she or wasn't she allergic to wasps' stings? She didn't know.

Tracy didn't know what to do next. It was getting dark fast, and she was very weak: she had been stung by many wasps, she had a leg she couldn't walk on, and been without food for days.

Again she looked at Tala. She had just rolled over, and now with her head sideways was looking at her, moaning from pain, expecting some help from Tracy.

Was her puppy dying already? Slowly, crawling on her knees, very worried, she went over to Tala and put some mud on her head.

Then suddenly, in the far distance, she heard voices.

"Holy smoke! I must get to the lake right away," Tracy cried out excitedly. "I hear people! I must start walking. I'll get a stick to lean on."

A little later, leaning on the stick she had found, with Tala straggling way behind her, she started walking again. It was very painful and she made very little progress. But she knew for certain it was only a matter of seconds now before she would see the lake! At each turn of the trail she lifted her throbbing head and scanned the trail ahead, expecting to see it. At each turn she thought she had, but it always turned out to be a cruel illusion.

Then suddenly, coming around a sharp corner, next to a large bush, in the distance, she saw Salmon Lake! She couldn't see the whole lake, of course, just a glimpse of it. Yet without any doubt, right in front of her, was Salmon Lake! With the last bit of strength left in her body, straggling and swaying as a toddler learning to walk, she finally stood in front of it.

It was the end of her odyssey!

Jubilant, not quite trusting her eyes, she turned her head to the left, then to the right, and then back to the left again to make sure she wasn't mistaken.

But despite her extreme pleasure at finally reaching the lake, she was a little disappointed as well. It wasn't at all what she had expected. She had expected a lake with wide sandy beaches (those you can easily walk on with bare feet), and toddlers playing in the water with multicoloured balls and little sail boats, all glittering in the sunshine. But that wasn't the case at all. Instead, the shore was rocky, bleak and inhospitable, covered with slippery boulders, dead trees, and branches black from many centuries of decay.

Rather discouraged by what she was seeing, she sat down on one of the boulders and looked for boaters. To her immense relief she spotted several almost immediately. Most were far, far away, on the opposite side of the lake, hardly visible. But one, a small sail boat, was rather close; so close even that she could see the boaters, and overhear snippets of their conversation. To Tracy's great excitement the boat was heading straight towards her!

Her rescue she expected, was imminent, only seconds away!

But had the boaters seen her? Probably not yet. She must start signalling right away. She tried to get right to the lakefront to be as visible as possible, but couldn't. The boulders along the lake were too steep and slippery, far too dangerous to climb over.

Then Tracy tried to climb on top of the boulder she was sitting on, but couldn't do that either. Her legs were too sore. Even the leg that wasn't sprained had abandoned her. Then she cried for help, hoping that the boaters would hear her. But her throat was too swollen; her cries sounded like whispers, hardly audible. Then, in desperation, she tried to lift the stick that had supported her in the air to start signalling. But even for that she lacked the strength.

Fixated, as if seeing a ghost approaching, she watched the boat get nearer and nearer. A little later it was so close that she could see the boaters, a man and a woman.

Had they seen her?

Suddenly it was all over! The boat started to change course. It was sailing away from her. They hadn't see her!

It was more than Tracy could bear!

Everything went black before her eyes.

She passed out.

# Chapter 7

It was Tala who saved Tracy's life! After Tracy had passed out, Tala ran to the waterfront and started barking without interruption as loud as she could in the direction of the turning sail boat.

And the boaters heard her.

They were quite surprised to hear the barking of a dog there, on that lonely shore, hardly ever visited by anyone! There wasn't even a proper beach - just slippery rocks, dead trees, and smelly weeds. How did that dog get there? Was it lost? Why was it barking so? Was its owner in trouble, was he hurt perhaps?

Turning their boat towards the shore, they decided to find out.

Only when they had reached the shore did the barking stop. Suspecting that something was wrong, very wrong, they left their boat, and started to investigate.

They first spotted Tala. She was lying behind a rock, bleeding badly and in great pain. When they talked to her, she tried to get up, but couldn't. The boaters then realised that something traumatic had happened to her, and decided to get to the bottom of it. They looked around to see if they could find the owner. Perhaps he was in trouble, perhaps hurt as well!

It was the woman who first spotted Tracy. Horrified by what she saw, she rushed over to her, closely followed by her husband. Tracy was lying beside a rock, motionless. She was covered in mud from her head down to her feet. Her face was badly swollen and her clothes torn as if a wild animal had attacked her. Had it been a bear or cougar perhaps? The woman spoke to Tracy, but she didn't respond. The boaters then realised that the girl immediately needed medical help!

While the woman stayed with Tracy, the man ran back to his boat and called the Salmon Lake Emergency Service. A short while later a rescue helicopter arrived and the medics wrapped Tracy in a blanket, and took her to a hospital.

When Tracy finally opened her eyes, the first creature she saw was Tala, curled up next to her and awake. Her nose was firmly resting on Tracy's chest, and with her brown eyes mostly hidden behind her long ears, she was watching Tracy.

Then Tracy noticed the nurse who was looking after her. She was sitting in a chair next to her, smiling broadly.

Straightening out her uniform a bit, the nurse said:

"Oh my dear, my dear . . . I'm so glad you're awake! How do you feel? You're in a hospital. When we took you in, my dear, you were, very weak, but now you're recovering nicely. You are looking much better already! Do you remember what happened at the lake, my dear? Is there anything you can remember? We'd like to know."

Tracy tried to please the nurse, but remembered very little. She did remember that a sail boat had come towards her with two people in it, a man and a woman; and that at the last moment it had changed course. But what had happened next, she couldn't remember! She must have passed out.

A little later, though, she must have regained consciousness again. She remembered the loud swishing of the rotors of a helicopter. She also remembered that someone had wrapped her in a blanket and carried her away.

That was all she could remember.

Exhausted from trying to recall the events, Tracy closed her eyes again, and fell asleep.

A few hours later Tracy's parents and Bonny arrived. Tracy's dad then told Tracy that they, of course, had been extremely worried about her. They had been much relieved when they received a message from the Salmon Lake Emergency Service that she, with her dog, had been found on the shore of Salmon Lake, and that they now were in the hospital, and that both were recovering nicely.

Her father then told Tracy all that had happened after she had left Bonny behind on the trail to fetch Tala. Bonny had waited about an hour, getting increasingly worried as time went by. At last, she had rushed back to the campsite to get help. Then he, together with Bonny, had gone back to the trail to try to find the place where Tracy had left Bonny. Unfortunately, Bonny hadn't paid much attention to the path, so she couldn't remember where it was.

They then had left the trail at several likely locations to search for her, Tracy's father continued, calling out her name as loud as they could. But there had been no reply. As it was getting dark, they finally were forced to return to the campsite. There, they had immediately contacted the local Search and Rescue Officers. Early the following day, a Search and Rescue plane had started searching for her, but they had not been able to locate her.

Finally her father told her that it was her dear puppy who had saved her life. Had Tala not barked so persistently in the direction of the boaters after Tracy had passed out, they would never have turned around.

When Tracy heard *that*, she slowly turned over to Tala, wrapped her arms around her, and started to cry.

"What? . . .Tala? . . . You? . . . You . . . saved my life?"

With shame Tracy remembered the many times she had been quite cross at her. Even at one time almost gave her a mushroom with red spots on it that could have killed her! And in the end . . . it was Tala who saved her life!

Just at that very moment Tala opened her eyes, looked at Tracy, stretched herself lazily, yawned once or twice, and went back to sleep again. She had to catch up on her sleep.

Did she harbour any ill feelings towards Tracy? Of course not!

Made in the USA
Columbia, SC
21 November 2017